DRAW
Grassland Animals

by

Doug DuBosque

Peel Productions, Inc.
GROWING BOOKS FOR GROWING PEOPLE!

10 9 8 7 6 5 4 2

Manufactured in the United States of America

Library of Congress Cataloging-in-Publication Data

DuBosque, Doug
    Draw grassland animals / by Doug DuBosque
            p. cm.
    Includes index.
    Summary: Offers step-by-step instructions for drawing various
grassland animals.
    ISBN 0-939217-25-2 (paper)
    1. Grassland animals in art--Juvenile literature. 2. Drawing--
Technique--Juvenile literature. [Grassland animals in art. 2.
Drawing--Technique.] I. Title.
NC783.8.G73D83   1996
743'.6--dc20
                                    95-51692
                                    CIP

DRAW
Grassland Animals
— CONTENTS —

Introduction

The grasslands of the world – also known as savannas– contain creatures that will delight and amaze you with their size, speed, and behavior. They're fun, and challenging, to draw.

Draw Grassland Animals shows you how. Step by step instructions lead you from simple beginnings to impressive final results. This book will help you look, and then put what you see on paper. You don't need to be an artist to begin (but you might become one)!

Think of drawing in three stages. First you get all the shapes and pieces in the right place. Draw lightly at this stage! Next, you add details, textures, and shading. Finally, you make any adjustments to lines and tones, and 'clean up' any smudges with your eraser. The steps for creating each animal drawing are described as well as shown.

In these pages, I take you through all the stages. The first stage takes several drawings, as we draw lightly, putting the pieces together. The final drawing of each set shows a finished drawing, with details and shading added and the 'cleaning up' completed.

I think you'll be surprised by your own great drawings of grassland animals. Putting the pieces together, one step at a time, is much more rewarding than tracing!

Remember that practice makes all the difference…pick one drawing in the book that you really like. Then draw it over and over and over and over and over, following the steps I give or making up your own. Is the tenth drawing better than the first? How about the twentieth? The one hundredth? The–?

Have fun looking and drawing!

Doug Dubosque

Supplies

- **pencil** (any kind)
- **pencil sharpener**
- **eraser** (I like the kneadable type)
- **paper** (drawing paper erases best)
- **blending stump** if you want to do smooth shading (you can use your finger, too, but it's a bit messy)
- **place to draw**
- **POSITIVE ATTITUDE!**

Always draw lightly at first!

Giant Anteater

Myrmecophaga tridactyla
South America. Size: 1.5–2 m. (4–6 ft)
Inside that long snout is a long, sticky tongue which the anteater uses to lick up termites and ants. With its sharp claws, it rips open nests, and rapidly flicks its tongue in and out of its mouth to grab the insects. The anteater sleeps in the open, wrapping its hairy tail around its body to keep warm.

1) Draw three ovals, very lightly.

snout

eye   ear

2) Add the snout to the smallest oval. Draw the eye and ear. Draw the graceful, curving line of the tail from the top of the biggest oval. Make pencil strokes for the hair on the tail.

3) Draw the curving fronts of the two front legs. Create short pencil strokes for the hair on the back of the front legs. Add the claws, curving underneath the feet. Draw hair on the bottom of the body. Add the back legs, and shade the distinctive dark area under the neck. Add the distinctive band of dark fur back from the neck.

4) Finish the drawing by adding short pencil strokes and shading on the body. Watch the direction of the lines! Leave the front legs lighter.

Notice how shading can cover up the original ovals.

Nine-banded Armadillo

Dasypus novemcinctus
USA, Central & South America. Size: 70–90 cm (27.5–35.5. inches) including tail. Guess how many bands of plates this armadillo has? Answer: between eight and eleven (good news if you're not a careful drawer!). At night, it digs with its clawed forefeet to find insects, spiders, small reptiles and amphibians in holes and crevices. During the day, it sleeps in its burrow, often with several other armadillos.

tail

1) Draw a horizontal oval, with two lines at one end to form a thick tail.

2) Add a rounded, *tapering* (thinner at one end) rectangle for the head. Draw the front and rear leg, with their sharp claws.

head

3) Add ears to the head. Draw a line for the top of the armored part of the head (see final drawing). Add the eye.

Draw the front and rear legs on the far side of the armadillo.

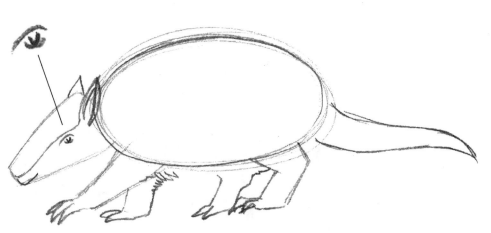

Always draw lightly at first!

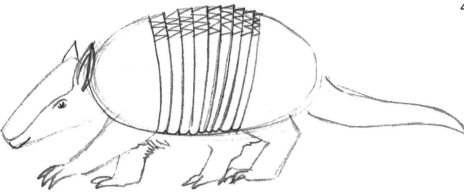

4) From top to bottom of the armadillo's body, draw the nine bands which give it its name. At the top, make them stick out a little from the outline of the body.

Does your drawing have to have exactly nine bands?

5) Inside each band, carefully add a zigzag line.

Add some short pencil strokes for fur on the face, legs, and body. Shade the legs on the far side of the body. Add a shadow on the ground.

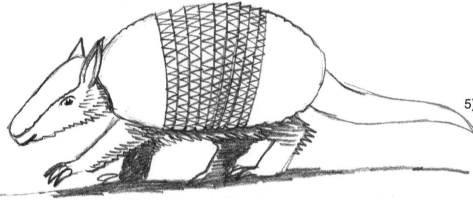

6) To finish your armadillo, simply add more and more narrow bands to the body, and fill each with rounded 'plates.' Do the same on the head and tail.

Awesome armadillo!

Olive Baboon

Papio anubis
Africa. Size, with tail: up to 1.5 m (5 ft).
Baboons live in troops of 20 to 150,
finding safety at night in trees or rocks.
They have strong jaws, and are
omnivorous: they eat grass, seeds,
roots, insects, birds' eggs and small
animals.

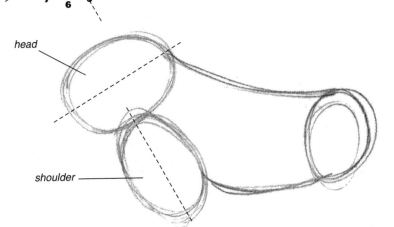

1) Draw a light oval for the hip
   of the baboon. From it,
   make two curving lines, one
   for the belly and one for the
   back. Look at the clock face
   to make sure your lines are
   running in the right direction.

2) Very lightly, add two more
   ovals—one for the head,
   and one for the shoulder.
   Again, look at the clock face
   to see the direction of the tilt
   of each oval.

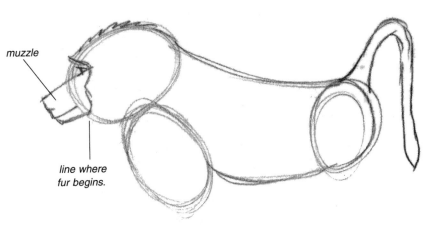

3) Add the tail, pointing almost
   straight up and then
   hanging back down. Add the
   muzzle (very much like a
   dog's muzzle), with nostril,
   mouth, eye, and the line
   where the fur begins.

4) Shade the muzzle, and add
   short pencil strokes to
   create the effect of fur,
   following the lines of the
   body. Shade the tail. Add the
   ear.

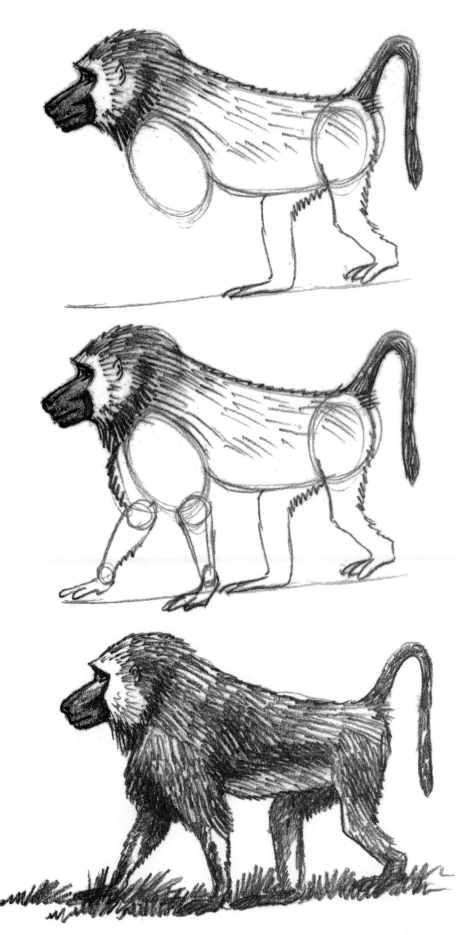

5) From the hip, draw the rear leg and foot closest to you, then add the other. Draw a light line for the ground.

6) From the bottom of the shoulder oval, lightly draw the front legs and feet. Use very light circles to remind you where they bend.

7) Finish your drawing by adding short pencil strokes for fur over the whole body, except for patches on the arms and legs. Look carefully at the directions the fur runs, and pay close attention to lighter and darker areas. Add scribbly lines for grass—grass is great for covering up feet that don't work out well!

Clean up any smudges with your eraser.

Bison

Bison bison
North America. Size: 2.6–4.1 m including tail; up to 2.9 m (9.5 ft) high at shoulder. Bison live in herds, which used to number in the millions. Early European settlers slaughtered so many that they almost became extinct by the early 20th century. Bison are grazers.

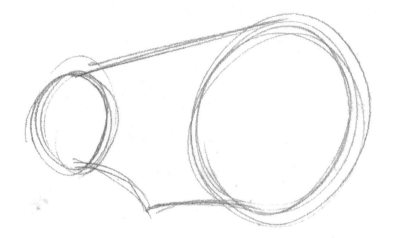

1) Draw two ovals, almost circular. Make one much larger than the other. Draw a straight line for the back of the bison, and a curved and straight line for its belly.

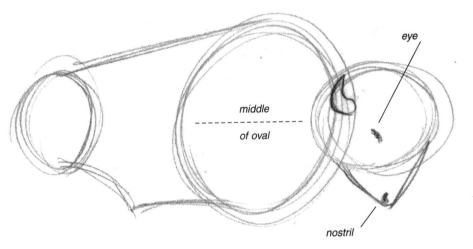

eye

middle
of oval

nostril

2) At the middle of the larger oval, draw a smaller oval for the head. Add the triangular front part of the head, pointing downward. Draw the horn, eye, and nostril.

3) Using short pencil strokes, add fur to the head, neck, and back. Add the ear!

Always draw lightly at first!

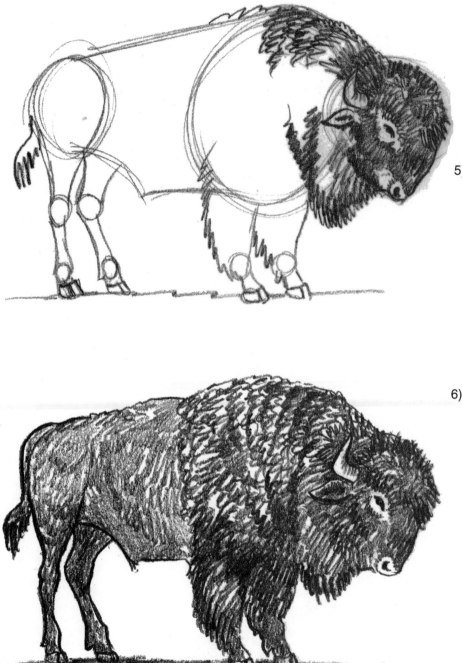

5) Before continuing with the fur, add the legs and tail. Draw the legs lightly, using small circles to emphasize the joints. Add a line for the ground.

Notice that the front legs are mostly covered with fur. The rear legs, however, require careful attention to details!

6) Now continue drawing the thick fur on the shoulder, back, and front legs. Lightly shade the rear portion of the bison. Thicken the cast shadow beneath the bison.

Clean up any smudges with your eraser.

Beautiful bison!

African Buffalo

Synceros caffer
Africa. Size: 2.8–4.1 m (9–13.5 ft) including tail. An aggressive animal, and dangerous to hunt–if wounded, it may wait in hiding to attack its hunter! Crocodiles and lions usually are able to kill only young or sick animals. It eats grass, bushes, and leaves.

1) Draw two almost-circular ovals. Make lines connecting the tops and bottoms as you see in the example.

2) Near the top of the larger oval, lightly sketch a circle for the head, then add the flat snout, eye, and horns. Draw the horns very lightly at first—you may need a couple of tries to get them right!

3) When you've got the horns looking right, add ears, nostrils, and mouth. With short pencil strokes, darken parts of the face. Add the curved tail.

4) Using small circles at the joints, sketch the legs. Pay close attention to the angle of each line. Make a light line for the ground to help you keep the legs the same length.

5) Add the other two legs in the same way.

6) Using short pencil strokes, shade the buffalo. You'll notice you don't have to completely shade the whole body—but also notice how dark the underside is. This *contrast* of light and dark suggests strong light overhead.

Draw some tall grass behind the African buffalo.

Looks kind of friendly, doesn't it? It's not!

Cheetah

Always draw lightly at first!

Acinonyx jubatus
Africa. Size: 1.7–2.2 m (5.5–7 ft) including tail. The cheetah is the fastest big cat. It can run at 112 km/h (69.5 mph) for short sprints. The cheetah hunts hares, jackals, small antelope, birds, and occasionally larger animals. After a quick chase, it knocks them down and kills them quickly by biting the throat .

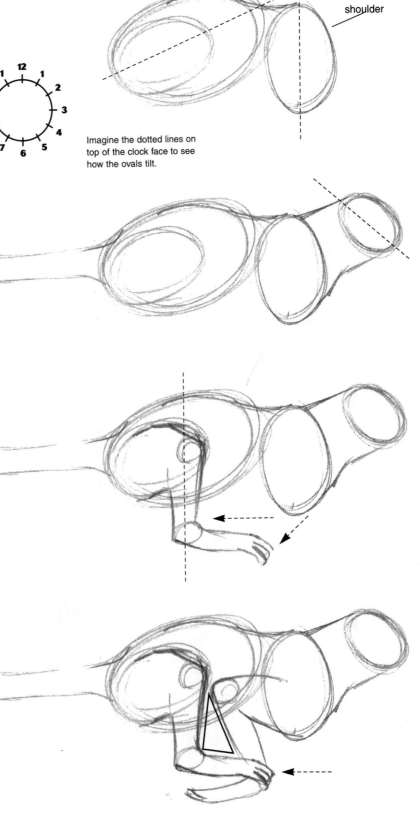

shoulder

Imagine the dotted lines on top of the clock face to see how the ovals tilt.

1) Draw a small oval, almost straight up and down, for the shoulder. Lightly sketch another, tilted oval for the body, and yet another inside it. Make a small line connecting the tops of the first two ovals.

2) Draw a tilted oval for the head. Draw two light lines to connect it to the body. Add the tail. Draw *lightly!*

3) Look carefully at the angles of the rear leg. The leg goes straight down from the front of the 'inside' oval. Where is the bend, compared to the first oval? How far forward does the paw reach?

Draw the rear leg.

4) Sketch the front leg, starting from the middle and the bottom of the shoulder oval. Look at the space between the legs as you draw, and notice how the front leg aligns with the rear paw.

14 **Draw Grassland Animals**

Always draw lightly at first!

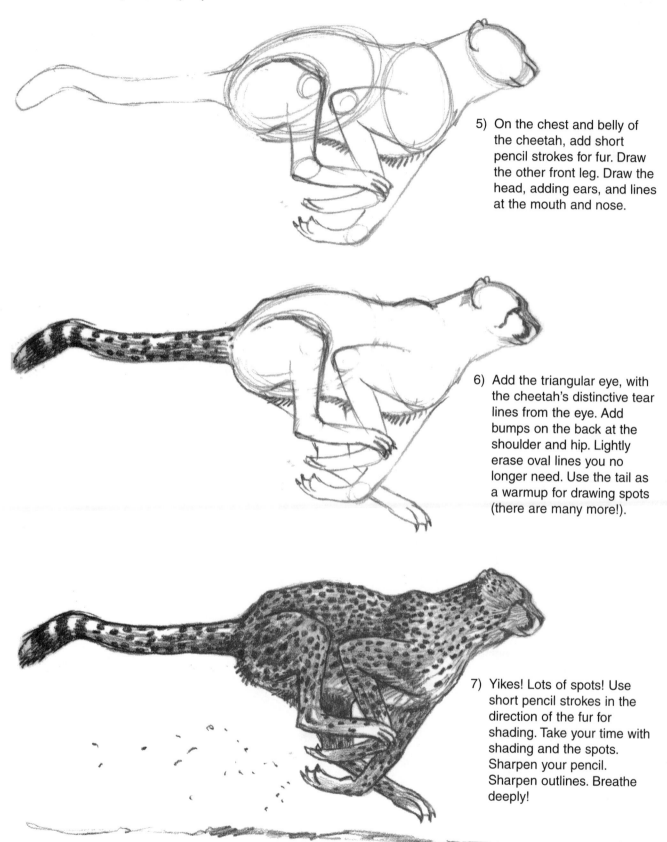

5) On the chest and belly of the cheetah, add short pencil strokes for fur. Draw the other front leg. Draw the head, adding ears, and lines at the mouth and nose.

6) Add the triangular eye, with the cheetah's distinctive tear lines from the eye. Add bumps on the back at the shoulder and hip. Lightly erase oval lines you no longer need. Use the tail as a warmup for drawing spots (there are many more!).

7) Yikes! Lots of spots! Use short pencil strokes in the direction of the fur for shading. Take your time with shading and the spots. Sharpen your pencil. Sharpen outlines. Breathe deeply!

Finally, clean up any smudges with your eraser.

Hunting Dog

Lycaon pictus
Africa. Size: 6–9 m (24–30 inches) high at shoulder. These scruffy hunters range widely, ferociously attacking but then letting the youngest pups eat first, and injured dogs as well. They are not closely related to domestic dogs.

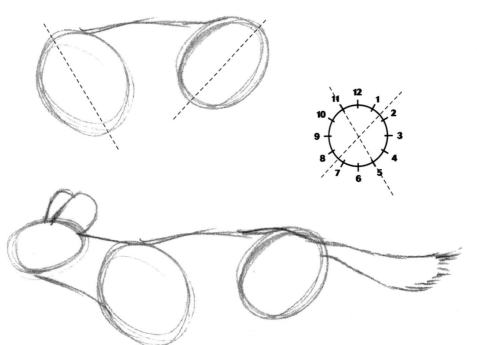

1) Start with two tilted ovals. Look at the clock face to make sure you have the right angle for the tilt of the ovals. Connect them at the top with a curving line for the back.

2) Lightly draw an oval for the head. Add ears. Draw lines to form the neck. Sketch the tail.

3) Draw the snout, lower jaw, and eye. With a sharp pencil, make short pencil strokes to 'map out' the direction of the fur on the face, neck, and ears.

4) Look carefully at the legs closest to you. You may find it helpful to make ovals at each joint—just draw them lightly! Draw the top of the front leg, then a longer, narrower section extending downward, ending with a different angle at the paw.

Now sketch the sections of the back leg, carefully looking at the example. Does the back leg touch the ground?

5) Look carefully at the sections of the legs farther from you. Drawing those little ovals at the joints can really help get the legs right. Notice that you don't see the entire leg.

Add a line for the ground, and spots for dirt kicked up by the running dog.

6) One difference between an OK drawing and a truly awesome drawing is slowing down for details at the end, shading, and cleaning up. Sharpen your pencil, and draw light, short lines to show the direction of the fur. Look closely at my example if you don't have your own hunting dog nearby. Add some low grass.

Since the one front leg is bearing the weight of the dog, give it a little added emphasis.

Sharpen your pencil again, and go over the entire drawing, from nose to tail, ear to toe, darkening fur to give the dog its characteristic scruffy look. Don't be scared to get some lead out of that pencil…just make sure you have a sharp point when you sharpen lines and work on the fur.

African Elephant

Loxodonta africana

Africa. Size: 7–9 m. Elephants can consume up to 200 kg (440 lbs) of plants a day, making them sometimes unwelcome neighbors where people grow food. African elephants have bigger ears and tusks than Indian elephants, and two finger-like extensions at the end of the trunk.

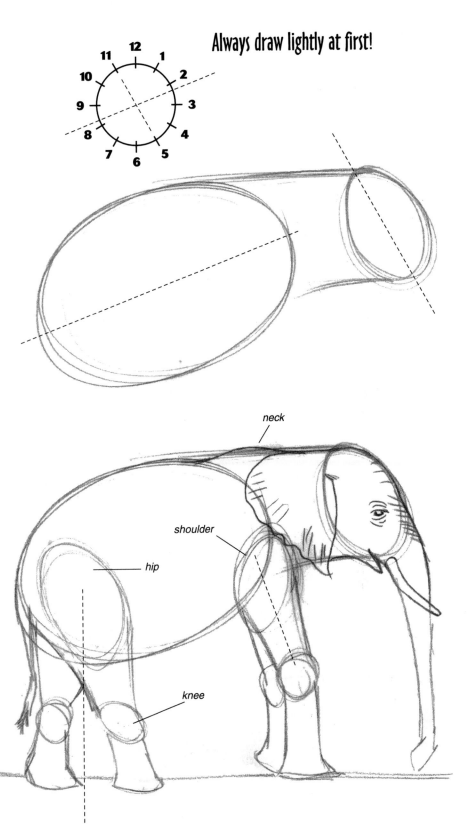

1. *Before you draw, use the clock face to identify the angles of the two ovals you will draw first.*

   Start with a large oval for the body of the elephant. Add a smaller oval for the head.

   Does the head oval touch the oval of the body? How much space is between them?

   Lightly sketch lines to connect the body and head.

2. Look carefully at the angle of each leg. *Does any leg go straight up and down?*

   LIghtly draw a line for the ground. Draw the legs, very lightly at first, using ovals for the knees, as well as the hip and shoulder. From the sides of the head oval, draw gently curving lines for the trunk, reaching almost to the ground.

   Where the trunk joins the head, add a tusk and the mouth (not just a line!). Directly above that, draw the eye. Add a bump on the top of the neck. Draw the ear…notice that it covers much of the neck.

Always draw lightly at first!

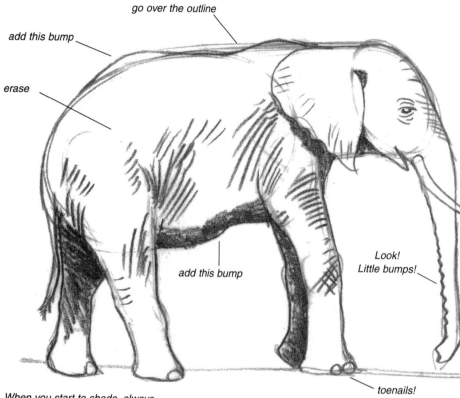

go over the outline

add this bump

erase

add this bump

Look!
Little bumps!

toenails!

When you start to shade, always look for the darkest areas first

3. First, complete the outline of the body: add a bump on the back and a small bump at the stomach. Add toenails! Go over the outline of the elephant, and carefully erase lines you don't need—for example, those ovals you started with.

Look at the final drawing, or look at a photo of an elephant. Study the wrinkles in the elephant's skin—zillions of them! Can you draw every single wrinkle? Probably not. What you can do is suggest wrinkles, by making plenty of lines running in the direction of the wrinkles.

Next, add lines showing the direction of the major wrinkles.

Now begin to shade, starting with the darkest parts of the drawing.

4. *How much white do you see on the final drawing? Not much! Since the elephant is gray, your whole elephant should be gray when you finish.*

Shade and shade and shade and shade! Use your wrinkle lines to show you which direction to make shading lines.

When you're satisfied with your drawing, look at it in a mirror—or through the back of the paper—to spot any last minute improvements you can make!

Draw Grassland Animals   **19**

Gerenuk

Litocranius walleri
Africa. Size: (body) 1.4–1.6 m (4.5–5.25 ft). Gerenuks are graceful gazelles distinguished by a long neck (gerenuk means 'giraffe-necked' in Somali). They eat leaves and shoots of thorny bushes and trees, which they're able to reach with their long legs and necks. They eat in the morning and evening, and spend the hottest part of the day standing still in the shade.

1) Draw two light ovals, and connect them at the top and bottom with curving lines.

2) Sketch two circles *(lightly, of course!)* for the head and nose. Add the eye, near the top of the head. Connect the head to the body with long, curving lines.

   How long is the neck, compared to the length of the body?

   Add the tail.

3) Draw the nose, mouth, and jaw line. Add horns and ears. Following the example, add shading on the head and ears.

   Using circles at the joints, draw the long, slender legs. The front leg goes almost straight up and down, but not the rear leg: notice how it extends *beyond* the back of the body.

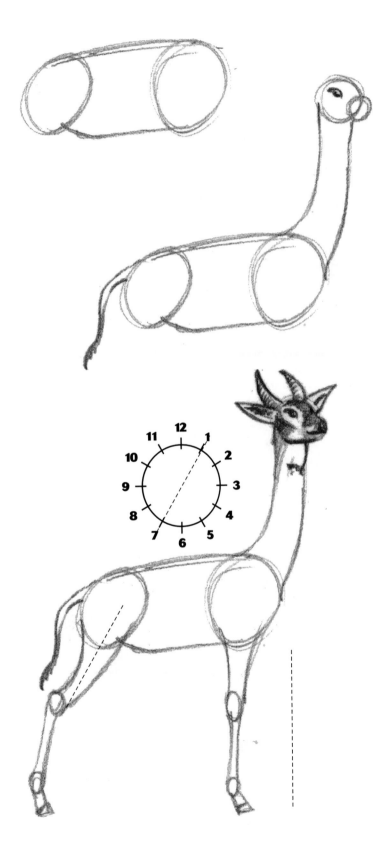

4) Add the other two legs. Go over the outline, using thinner and thicker lines to make it more interesting and emphasize the structure of the body.

5) With short pencil strokes, shade the body. The gerenuk is darkest on top, lighter brown along the side, and white underneath.

Add a background with acacia trees...!

Graceful gerenuk!

Where do you suppose the name Gerenuk *comes from?*

Giraffe

Giraffa camelopardalis
Africa. Size: 3.3 m (11 feet) high at shoulder, nearly 6 m (19.5 ft) at crown. Giraffes live in small groups. They eat foliage and fruit from the tops of acacia and thorn trees.

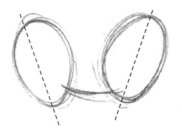

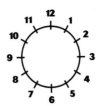

1) Lightly draw two ovals, tilted slightly outward. Use the clock face to help see the correct angles. Connect the ovals with a small curved line on the bottom.

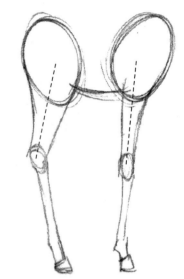

2) Draw the two legs closest to you, using small ovals at the joints. Notice how the rear leg is larger at the top, and how its angles are different than the front leg.

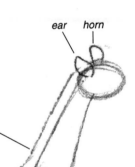

3) Add the two legs further from you. Draw them lightly at first, so that you can change them if you need to—notice I had to adjust the length of the legs at the hooves; fortunately, these get fairly well hidden by grass in the final step!

   Draw the tail.

4) Make a light oval for the head, far above the body. Add the angled lines of the neck. Draw a light line for the back. Sketch the outline of the mane, ear, and horn.

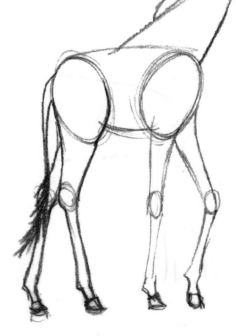

ear   horn

mane

Always draw lightly at first!

5) Draw the front of the head, with nose and mouth. Make a horizontal line with a curved line below it for the eye, with another curved line above for the eyelid. Use short pencil strokes to create the mane. Go over the whole outline to refine it.

Lightly erase the ovals and any other lines you no longer need.

6) Study the pattern on the giraffe before drawing it. Note that most of the dark patches are four-sided, but not square. After you draw the patches on the giraffe, add a little shading to help emphasize the form (roundness) of the animal. Make some short pencil strokes for grass. Finish up by cleaning any smudges with your eraser.

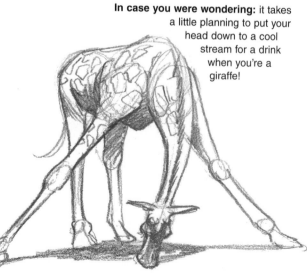

In case you were wondering: it takes a little planning to put your head down to a cool stream for a drink when you're a giraffe!

Spotted Hyena

Crocuta crocuta
Africa. Size: 1.5–2.1 m (±5–7 ft) with
tail. Hyenas are mostly active at night.
Like vultures, they quickly clean up
carrion (dead animals) and so help
prevent the spread of disease from
rotting flesh. The spotted hyena looks
like a strong dog, and is found south of
the equator in Africa .

Always draw lightly at first!

1) Draw two light *overlapping*
   ovals, and connect them
   with *concave* curving lines.
   Notice the different tilt of
   each oval. (Compare the
   axis of each oval with the
   clock face.)

2) Draw another *very light* oval
   for the shoulder. Draw light
   ovals where the legs bend,
   then draw the upper legs,
   lower legs, and paws.

3) Draw small ovals for the
   ankles on the back leg. Add
   the upper and lower legs,
   and rear paws. Use short
   pencil strokes to draw the
   tail.

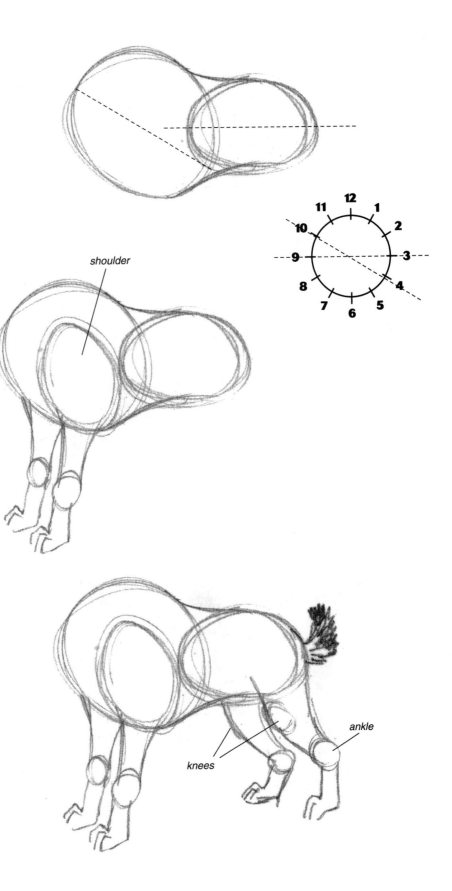

shoulder

knees

ankle

Always draw lightly at first!

back of neck

throat

4) Draw a *light* circle, touching the large oval you drew in step one, for the head. Add two partial circles for ears. Lightly sketch lines for the throat and back of neck.

5) At the bottom of the head, draw the nose and mouth. Next, toward the center of the circle, draw the eyes (notice they're at an angle to each other). Add whiskers, and shading around the face and neck.

6) Go over the outline, making it jagged where fur stands out. (Look carefully at the final drawing.) Start at one end and add shading and spots. Draw a *cast shadow* underneath on the ground. Clean up any smudges with your eraser.

Is your drawing perfect? If not, think about trying it again—or hold your drawing up to a mirror, or look at it through the back of the paper to see areas that need improvement.

Red Kangaroo

Macropus rufus

Central Australia. Size: 1.9–2.7 m (6.25–8.75 ft) including tail. Kangaroos stay in shady places during the day, and feed in the evening. Kangaroos are marsupials, meaning the young crawl into a pouch after birth. They stay there about 240 days.

Always draw lightly at first!

1) Look at the angles of these ovals! Now, draw an oval for the top of the leg, and around it a larger—very light!—oval for the largest part of the body. Draw two vertical lines for the legs, and then add the horizontal part of the leg with foot.

2) From the large oval, draw the tail, angling down toward the ground and then laying flat on it. Add the bit of the other leg that's visible, and begin the pouch where the joey (baby kangaroo) will peek its head out.

Draw another very light oval for the shoulder, with lines connecting it to the rear part of the body.

3. Draw a light oval for the head. Add two lines for the neck. Draw the snout, with nose, mouth, and chin. Lightly draw the two ears, and the eye.

Always draw lightly at first!

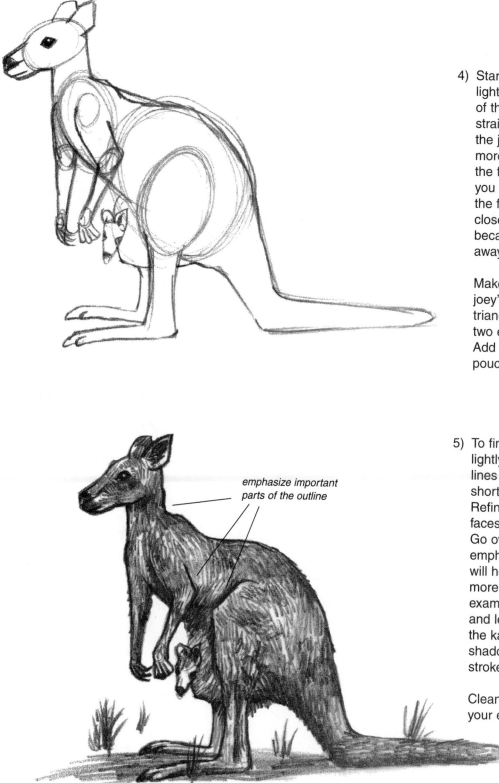

emphasize important
parts of the outline

4) Starting at the shoulder, lightly draw the 'mechanics' of the arm, using light straight lines and ovals at the joints (of course you see more of the closer arm than the farther arm). Notice that you can see the claws on the farther arm, but on the closer arm you can't, because they're pointing away from you.

Make a light triangle for the joey's head, with two little triangular shapes for eyes, two ears, and a dark nose. Add lines to complete the pouch.

5) To finish your drawing, lightly erase unnecessary lines and fill in the body with short pencil strokes for fur. Refine details (particularly faces) with a sharp pencil. Go over the outline, adding emphasis where you think it will help make the drawing more interesting (for example, where the arm and leg overlap the side of the kangaroo). Add a subtle shadow and some pencil strokes for grass.

Clean up any smudges with your eraser. Kool kangaroo!

Kangaroos travel in herds called mobs, with about a dozen members. Draw a mob of kangaroos—try drawing them them in different positions!

Draw Grassland Animals   **27**

Kudu

Tragelaphus strepsiceros
Africa, introduced in N. Mexico. Size: 2.1.–3 m including tail. This attractive antelope feeds on leaves, shoots and seeds. The male has the long, spiraling horns, which lay flat along the back when he's running. Females sometimes have short horns.

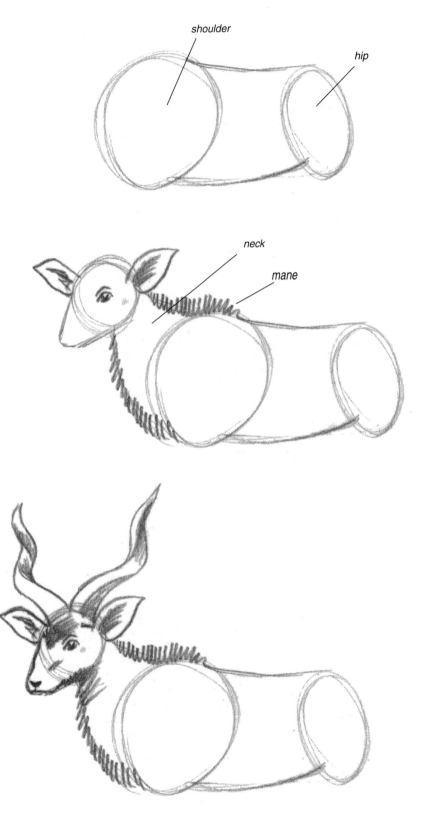

1) Start with two lightly drawn ovals. Make one (the shoulder) large and almost round. Make the other (the hip) smaller, skinnier, and slightly tilted. Connect the ovals with a *concave* line on the top, and a *convex* line on the bottom.

   Where do these lines connect to the ovals?

2) First, look: *how much space is there on the neck, between the shoulder and the head?* Draw a very light circle for the head. Add the bulge of the nose. Carefully draw the eye and the ears. Add curving lines for the neck, with short vertical pencil strokes for the mane and the bottom of the neck.

3) Draw curved lines for the horns, joining to make points at the end. Carefully apply shading to create the spiralling effect.

   Add the nose, mouth, and shading on the head.

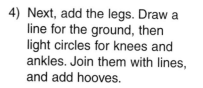

4) Next, add the legs. Draw a line for the ground, then light circles for knees and ankles. Join them with lines, and add hooves.

Add the tail.

5) Starting with the darkest areas, carefully shade the entire body. Watch for shadows on the neck and shoulder, representing muscles. Try to leave the white stripes on the back as you shade; you may be able to create them after with your eraser.

Go over the outline, adding emphasis. Clean up any smudges.

This final shading may take some time, but will certainly earn you kudos for your kudu!

Lion (female)

Panthera Leo

Africa (south of Sahara), Northwest India. Size: 2–3 m (6.5–10 ft) including tale. The male is larger, with a heavy mane. Lions spend 20 hours or more resting each day. The females hunt gazelles, antelope, and zebras, and sometimes cooperate to kill larger prey like buffaloes and giraffes. Like other cats, they stalk their prey and capture it with a short, quick chase. The males rarely hunt.

1) Draw a vertical oval for the hip. Now, look: *how much space is there between this oval and the shoulder?* Draw the tilted shoulder oval (refer to the clock face for the angle). Add gracefully curving lines to connect them. Draw the tail.

2) Draw a light circle for the head, overlapping the shoulder oval. Add ears.

   Below the shoulder, draw a light circle for the front knee. Add lines upward for the top of the leg, and down for the bottom of the leg, ending with the foot and paws. Now draw the other front leg.

   Draw the rear legs, starting with circles for the ankles (the knee is not as important in this pose—look at the male lion drawing to see the rear knee).

3) Study the features of the face, and draw eyes, nose, mouth, and whiskers.

4) Carefully add shading over the entire body, watching for light and dark areas. Add the ground with a few tufts of grass.

Always draw lightly at first!

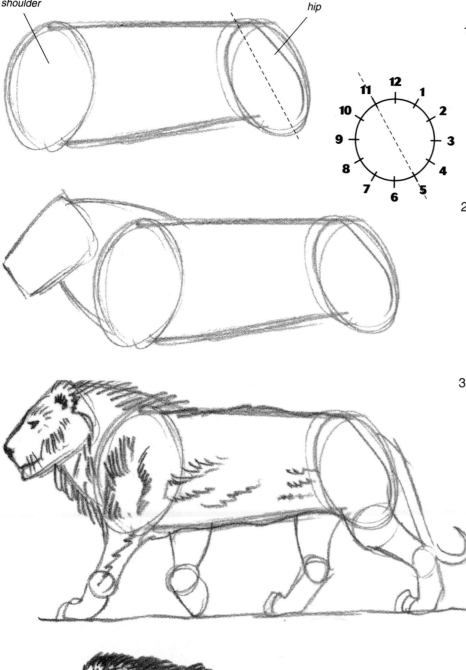

shoulder

hip

12
11 1
10   2
9   3
8   4
7 6 5

1) Draw a titled oval for the lion's hip. Being careful to leave enough space for the body, draw the shoulder oval, and lines to connect the two ovals. *Where do they connect to each oval?*

2) Draw the boxy shape of the lion's head, slightly smaller at the mouth end. Notice the angles of the box. Add curving lines for the top and bottom of the neck. *Where do they connect to the body?*

3) Draw a line for the ground, and use light circles and lines to 'map out' the legs. Pay close attention to the angles, and look at the shapes between the legs (*negative space*) as well as the shapes of the legs themselves.

Add nose, mouth, eye, and ear. Use short pencil strokes for whiskers, mane, bottom of neck and at places on the body where muscles show.

4) Continue shading, emphasizing muscles. Leave contrast between light and dark to suggest strong light. Go over the outline, especially on the legs.

Clean up with your eraser.

Locust

Locusts thrive on every continent. They are the most destructive member of the grasshopper family—a large swarm can eat 3,000 **tons** of crops each day. No wonder they've been considered a plague since early times! Though locusts can be controlled with pesticides, that raises another problem: locusts provide food for other animals, including storks and rodents.

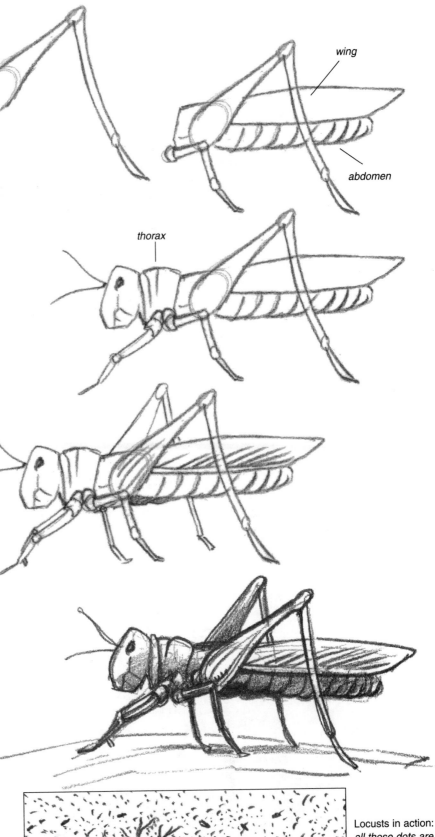

1) Start your locust drawing with the hind leg. It looks somewhat like the leg of a mammal, such as a gazelle, but it bends the opposite way.

2) Add the wing and abdomen, as well as the next leg.

3) Draw the thorax and head (notice where the eye is), antennae and front leg.

4) Add the three legs on the far side of the insect, plus lines on the largest leg and the wing.

5) Shade the locust, paying attention to which areas are darkest and which are lighter.

Arthropod appetizers:

Lightly saute with a little olive oil and salt to taste. Cook until slightly crunchy.

Delicious!

Locusts in action: *all those dots are locusts. Very little vegetation remains after they've passed through an area.*

Burrowing Owl

Speotyto cunicularia
North, Central and South America.
Size: 23–28 cm (9–11 inches). The burrowing owl lives in abandoned burrows of prairie dogs and other mammals, digging out a nesting area with its feet. Its short tail and long legs are well-suited for ground dwelling. They like to follow moving dogs or horses, to catch insects and other small prey disturbed by the larger animal.

1) Draw a long, tilted oval for the owl's body. Compare the angle of the tilt with the clock face. Above the body, draw a horizontal oval, and connect it to the body with curving lines. Add the squared off section of tail feathers at the bottom.

2) Next draw the face, starting with the beak. Add two lines slanting upward for the eyebrows, with partial circles underneath for the eyes. Draw other details, noticing how they *radiate* from the eyes, adding emphasis to them.

   Add long lines for the wing feathers.

3) Using light circles for the joints, draw the legs, and toes with sharp claws.

4) Darken the eyes, leaving a small bright spot in one (this helps make the owl look alive!). Carefully add shading over the body. Toward the head, white spots appear on a darker background. Toward the tail, darker patterns appear on a light background.

   Add a burrow in the background. You can smear the pencil a bit to contrast with the sharp detail of the owl's face.

Meerkat

Suricata suricatta
Southern Africa. Size: 45–55 cm
(1.5–1.8 ft) including tail. The meerkat,
also known as the suricate, has thin fur
on its belly. When it wants to get
warmer, it sits up so the sun warms its
belly. When it wants to cool off, it lies
belly-down in a cool, dark burrow.
Meerkats eat all kinds of food, mostly
animal. Cute as they appear, you
wouldn't want one for a pet: they're
messy and they don't smell very nice!

1) Draw two tilted ovals, for the
   hip and shoulder. Use the
   clock face to check the tilt of
   each oval. Connect the two
   ovals with slightly *concave*
   curving lines.

2) Touching the lower left edge
   of the hip oval, draw a small
   circle for the meerkat's
   knee. Below the hip oval,
   draw another small circle at
   the ankle. Connect these
   circles and the body with
   curving lines. From the
   ankle, draw the lower part of
   the leg, and the foot.

3) Using similar circles, draw
   the arm (front leg). Add the
   small bit that shows of the
   other leg and arm.

4) Draw a light circle for the
   head, and extend it to make
   the nose. Add curving lines
   for the neck. Draw ears, eye,
   and mouth.

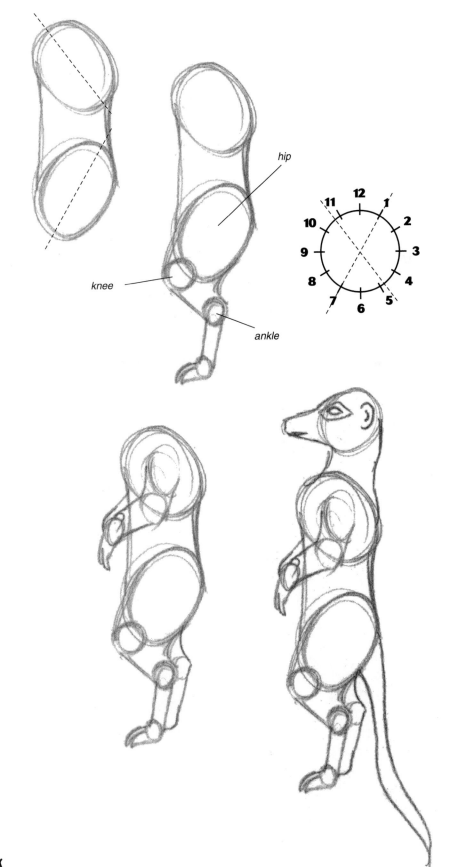

5) Add the nose and whiskers. Sharpen your pencil and go over the outline, adding jagged lines where fur sticks out.. Lightly sketch the second meerkat, and lines for the ground.

(Why might one be standing when the other is lying down?)

6) Add short pencil strokes in the direction of the fur, except in parts of the body which remain light. Add the distinctive bands, or stripes, on the back.

Clean up any smudges with your eraser.

Magnificent meerkats!

If at first you don't succeed…

Black-tailed prairie dog

Cynomys ludovicianus
(Black tailed prairie dog)
Central USA. Size: 36.5–41.5 cm
(14.2–16 inches) including tail.
Surprise! Prairie dogs aren't
dogs…they're sociable rodents who live
in burrows. They get their name from
their appearance and barking sound.
They eat grass and other plants. They
form part of the diet of hawks, foxes,
ferrets and coyotes.

1. *Draw very lightly!* Draw two
   ovals, one for the body and
   one for the head. Add a
   short curving line for the top
   of the neck.

2. Add the bottom of the neck
   and the front leg, with claws.
   Use light, wispy lines to
   draw the tail.

3. Draw a jagged line for the
   edge of the burrow. Make it
   bumpy, like dirt thrown up by
   the prairie dog's digging.

4. Lightly add the front of the
   prairie dog's face. *Do any of
   the lines go straight up and
   down (vertical) or straight
   side to side (horizontal)?*

   When you have the shape
   of the face the way you want
   it, carefully erase the front
   part of the oval. Then mark
   where you want the ear and
   eye.

5. Using curving lines, draw
   the ear and eye. Add
   whiskers and short pencil
   strokes for fur.

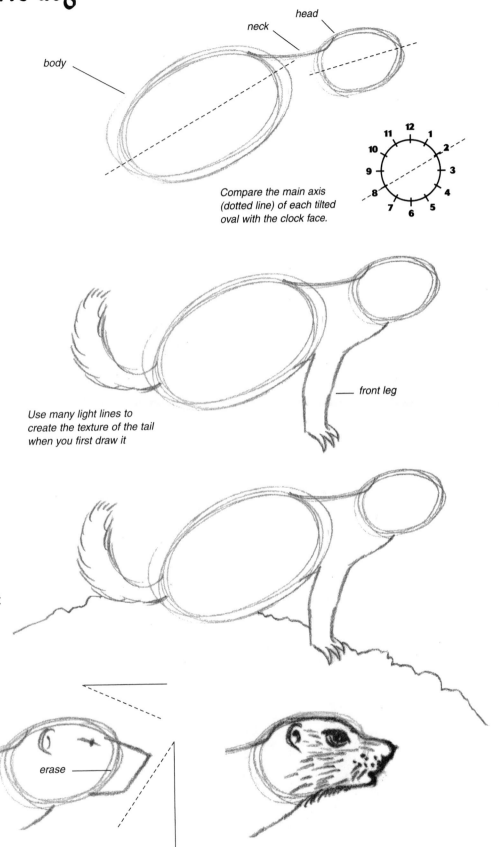

body

neck

head

Compare the main axis
(dotted line) of each tilted
oval with the clock face.

front leg

Use many light lines to
create the texture of the tail
when you first draw it

erase

Always draw lightly at first!

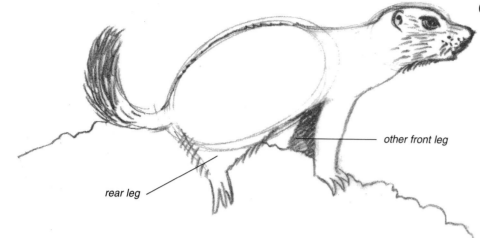

other front leg

rear leg

6. Add the other front leg, and shade it. Draw the rear leg. Go over the outline—notice how you can make it look more like fur by making the line a bit jagged. Add more short, curving pencil strokes to make the tail look furry. Carefully erase parts of the oval that you don't want in the finished drawing.

7. Look at the final drawing— where are the dark areas? These will be the areas we shade first. Use short pencil strokes going in one direction for the fur in the darkest parts of the body.

   Add a bumpy line for the dirt at the edge of the burrow closest to you. Use short pencil strokes going in different directions to shade the entrance to the burrow.

edge of burrow

8. Continue adding short pencil strokes for fur. Watch how they change direction on different parts of the body. Add more shading, rocks and grass. Clean up any smudges or "leftover" lines with your eraser.

   Now, what's that pretty prairie dog looking at?

Draw Grassland Animals

Pronghorn

Antilocapra americana
North America. Size: 1–1.7 m (3.5–5.5 ft). Pronghorn antelopes are fast runners and good swimmers. They eat grasses, weeds, and shrubs such as sagebrush.

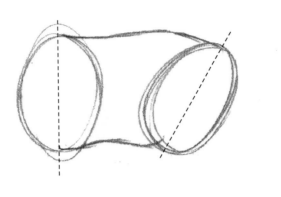

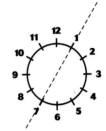

1) Draw two light ovals, one vertical and one tilted. Use the clock face to see how they tilt. Connect the tops and bottom with slightly curving lines. Note the bit of a hump at the hip, and bit of an indent underneath.

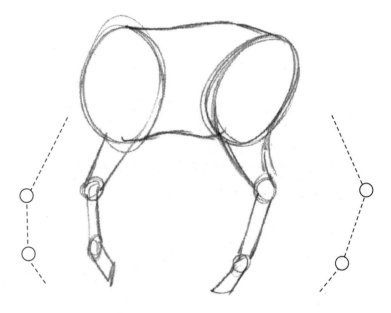

2) Sketch light lines and ovals to plot out how the legs bend. Pay special attention to the angles.

   Using the ovals at joints will help you see how the legs bend. Later, you may want to try putting the legs in different positions, perhaps using a photograph as a guide.

3) Add the other two legs. Draw a small oval for the head. Connect the head to the top of the body with a straight line *(look where it connects to the body!)*. Draw the bottom of the neck, with its two curves.

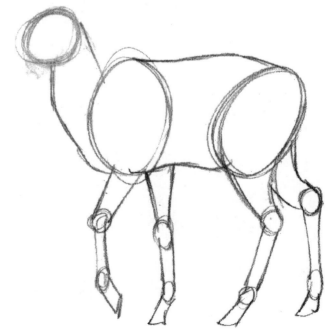

38   Draw Grassland Animals

Always draw lightly at first!

4) Add the snout, with nose and mouth. Draw the eye, high in the head. Add horns and ears.

   Lightly erase lines you no longer need. Sharpen your pencil and go over the outline of the animal, making your line thinner in some places and thicker in others. As you draw, you'll develop a feel for where to make lines thin and thick. Pay special attention to where lines meet or curve.

5) Being careful not to smudge your paper, add short pencil strokes for fur over the entire antelope. Leave the rump lighter. Also notice that part of the face and throat are lighter.

   This last step may take longer than all the ones leading up to it. Take your time!

   Clean up any smudges with your eraser.

Common Rabbit

Oryctolagus cuniculus
Europe, northwest Africa; introduced into other countries. Size: 39–52 cm (15–19.5 inches). This is the ancestor of the domestic rabbit. They live in underground colonies called warrens, and feed on grass and leaves, as well as bark and roots in winter. To warn other rabbits of danger, a rabbit may thump its foot.

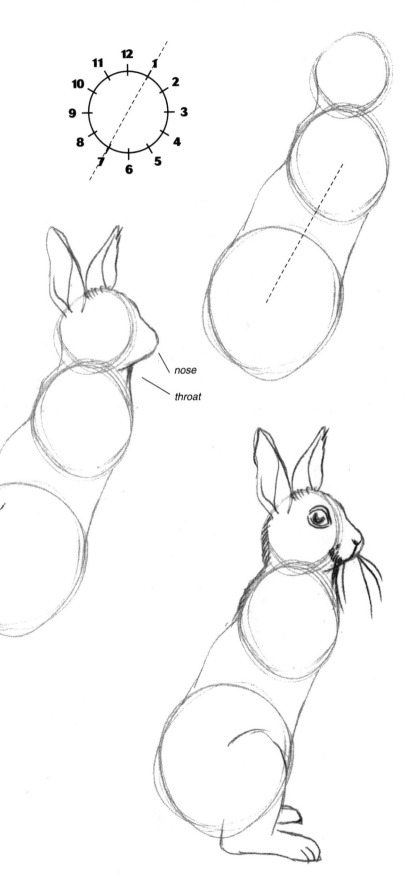

nose

throat

1) Start by lightly drawing three ovals. The top two touch. The bottom two don't touch—connect them with lines for the back and stomach of the rabbit.

2) Carefully—and *lightly!*— draw the ears. Add the rounded nose and the line for the throat.

3) Draw the eye, mouth and nose details, and whiskers. Add the feet.

Always draw lightly at first!

4) Draw the tail and front legs. Notice which are the darkest parts of the final drawing, and start to add shading there.

5) Complete your rabbit by filing the body with short pencil strokes for fur. Add grass. Go over any parts of the outline that might need additional emphasis or texture. Clean up any smudges with your eraser.

White Rhinoceros

Ceratotherium simum
Africa. Size: 3.6–5 m (12–16 ft). The only bigger land animal is an elephant! White rhinos are placid, and rarely attack, preferring to flee from trouble. They eat only grass. They're gray, not white—the name comes from their WIDE mouths, which are unlike pointy mouths of other rhinos.

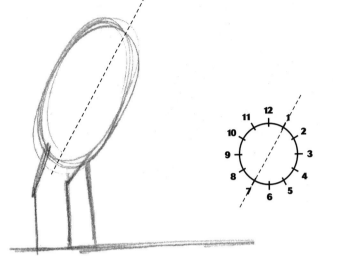

1) Lightly draw a tall, tilted oval for the rhino's hip. Look at the clock face to see the angle of the tilt. Add two bent lines showing the leg nearest you, and another straight line for the leg on the other side. Draw a line for the ground.

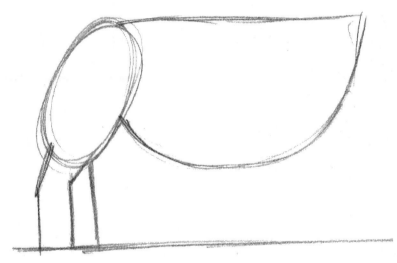

2) From the top of the oval, draw a horizontal line for the back, and a swooping, sagging line underneath for the belly. Extend the line for the ground.

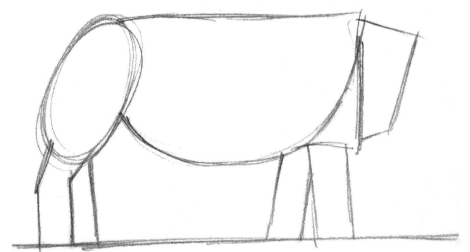

3) From the front of the body, draw a line straight down and back. Under it, add the front leg closest to you, then then one behind it. Sketch the shape for the neck.

Always draw lightly at first!

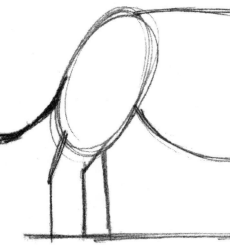

4. Draw a rectangle for the head, getting smaller towards the front. Add the two horns, and the tail.

5) Now you'll find many details to add as you refine the head: draw lightly at first, and observe carefully. Add the eye and arcs around it, below and behind the smaller horn. Make the front of the head bulge out slightly and add a nostril and wrinkles. Add curves to the bottom of the head and neck, and wrinkles. Draw the ears, and bulges at the top of the neck.

6) Look at this finished drawing. Add curves to the legs, widening them to make feet; draw toenails. Draw lines for the ribs, then shade with short pencil strokes. Make the bottom of the body and the inside of the far legs darker. Follow the direction of the wrinkles as you shade the face. Add grass, and an egret to keep the rhino company!

Clean up any smudges with your eraser.

A note about shading: if it doesn't look good, add more!

Saiga

Saiga tatarica
Central Asia. Size: body 1.2–1.7m
(4–5.5 ft). Saigas migrate through cold,
treeless, windswept plains. Their large
noses are thought to help them survive
by warming and adding moisture to the
air they breathe.

Always draw lightly at first!

1) Draw two ovals, connected
   by rounded lines.

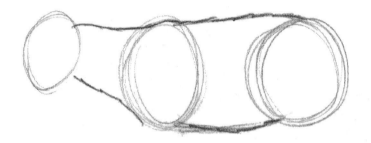

2) Add a third oval for the
   head, and draw lines for the
   neck. Notice where they
   connect to the oval for the
   head!

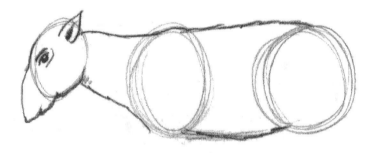

3) Draw the large nose, eye,
   and ear.

4) Using small circles at the
   joints, lightly draw the front
   and rear leg.

Always draw lightly at first!

5) Draw the remaining two legs.

6) Add the horns. Lightly erase the parts of the ovals you no longer need. Look carefully at the final drawing. Start shading with the face.

7) Continue shading with short pencil strokes to complete the Saiga. You can create a softer look by gently smudging part of the pencil drawing with your finger, a small rolled up piece of paper, or an artist's stump, which is made for that purpose.

Just be sure to wash your hands if you get graphite on them; they can make a mess of your picture fast!

Clean up any smudges with your eraser.

Secretary Bird

Sagittarius serpentarius
Africa. Size: 150 cm (59 inches). The secretary bird mostly walks, covering 30 km (20 miles) a day. It eats just about anything crawling on the ground. It either runs to catch it in its mouth, or stamps it with its foot. The odd name probably comes from the feathers on the head, which look like quill pens stuck behind the ear of a secretary in the old days.

Always draw lightly at first!

1) Draw a horizontal oval, with the two straight sections of leg extending downward from the middle of it.

   Notice the angle of each leg section—neither is perfectly vertical.

2) Add the second leg.

   Can you see the entire second leg?

3) Draw the front of the wing. Add the feet, each with four toes and sharp claws.

4) From the front of the wing, draw the triangular back part of the wing, with lines for feathers. Then add the feathers sticking out from underneath. Add shading.

second leg

front of wing

draw these feathers first...

...then these feathers.

5) Add the two long tail feathers. Add shading and jagged lines to fill out the bottom of the body. Shade the top part of the legs with short, dense, vertical pencil strokes. Go over the outline of the lower legs, and make evenly spaced horizontal marks on them.

Shade the feet. Draw a captured snake. Add the ground and grass.

6) Draw a small, horizontal oval for the head, and connect it to the front of the body with smoothly curved lines. Add the turned-down beak, eye and nose details, and distinctive 'quill' feathers.

7) Add short pencil strokes for neck feathers, shade the beak, head, and feathers. Clean up any smudges with your eraser.

Super Secretary bird!

Take a memo, please....

Draw Grassland Animals   **47**

Thomson's gazelle

Gazella thomsoni
Africa. Size: 1–2.3 m (3.25–7.5 ft)
including tail. Gazelles live in groups
and eat short grass. They need water
only when grazing is dry. They are prey
of lions, cheetahs, hunting dogs and
hyenas.

1) Draw a light circle for the
   hindquarters, and a smaller,
   vertical oval for the
   shoulder. Connect the two
   with slightly curved lines,
   and add the tail.

2) *Look: how much space do
   you need between the body
   and the circle for the head?
   Where is the head in
   relation to the body (see
   clock face)?*

   Lightly draw a circle for the
   head, and connect it to the
   body with curving lines. Add
   the eye and ears.

3) Extend the front of the circle
   for the gazelle's muzzle, and
   draw the the nose and
   mouth. Sketching very lightly
   at first—and rotating your
   paper if it helps—draw the
   horns, one partly covered by
   the other. add the pattern of
   dark fur inside the ear, and
   the dark patch extending
   toward the nose.

4) Using small ovals for the
   joints, draw the legs and
   hooves. Look carefully at the
   angles of each leg section.

hindquarters

shoulder

48 Draw Grassland Animals

Always draw lightly at first!

5) Draw a line for the ground, and add the other two legs. Notice the shading of the final drawing, and lightly sketch the curve on the rump that separates the lightest fur from the darker fur. Add the distinctive dark patch on the side.

Draw the wrinkles of the neck.

6) Using short pencil strokes in the direction of the fur, shade the entire body, except for the lightest parts. Go over the outline with a sharpened pencil, adding emphasis. Add ridges on the horns.

Try holding your drawing up to the light and looking at it through the back of the picture (or use a mirror)— do you notice any possible improvements you can make?

Clean up any smudges with your eraser.

Vicuña

Vicugna vicugna
South America. Size: 1.4–1.6 m (4.5–5.25 ft). Vicuñas live near the snow line in the Andes (above 4200 m; 14,000 ft). They avoid rocky places, because their hooves are soft and sensitive. The 'flag' of wool on the front is commercially valuable—in Inca times, only royalty were allowed to wear vicuña wool. Though gentle creatures, males defend their territory by biting and spitting regurgitated food.

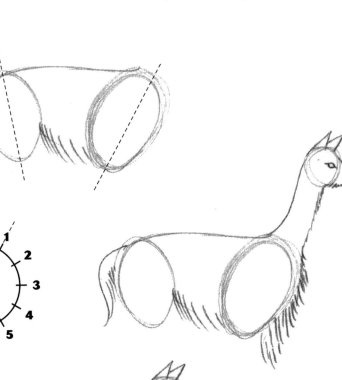

1) Draw two tilted ovals, referring to the clock face for the angle of the tilt. Add a curving line for the back, a curving tail, and long wispy pencil strokes for the fur on the belly.

2) Add a small, light circle for the head, and connect it with slightly curved lines for the neck. Extend the front of the head and add the nose and mouth. Draw the eye and ears. Add more long, wispy pencil strokes for the 'flag' of fur on the vicuña's breast.

3) Using small ovals at the joints, draw the legs. Notice the angles of different lines. Also notice that you don't have to draw much of the second rear leg!

4) Shade the vicuña with short pencil strokes. Concentrate first on getting the *values* (light and dark) right, then sharpen your pencil and add small lines to suggest texture. Go over the outline with a sharpened pencil, and add the shadow on the ground.

Clean up any smudges with your eraser.

Always draw lightly at first!

shoulder

12
11   1
10   2
9   3
8   4
7   5
6

foot

eyebrow

Plains viscacha

Lagostomus maximus
Argentina. Size: 62–86 cm (2–3 ft).
These large rodents live in complex,
underground burrows. They dig with
their forefeet and push soil out of the
way with their noses. How do they keep
dirt out of their noses? They close their
nostrils....

1) Draw a tilted oval for the
    shoulder. Add a light,
    rounder, larger oval near it,
    and draw curving lines at
    the top and the bottom of
    the body.

2) Draw a vertical oval,
    overlapping the shoulder
    slightly, for the head. Add
    the two ears. Below the
    shoulder, draw the front leg.
    Under the larger oval, draw
    the horizontal rear foot.
    Sketch the tail with short,
    outward pencil strokes.

3) Draw the eye, then a bump
    for the eyebrow. Extend the
    front of the head, and add
    the nose and mouth. Draw
    the inside of the ear, and
    wrinkles on the chin. Add
    the little visible bit of the
    other two legs. Now go over
    the outline with a sharpened
    pencil.

4) Using short pencil strokes,
    shade the body of the
    viscacha, leaving a light
    patch on the bottom and the
    tail. Pay close attention to
    the markings on the face.
    Add whiskers, and a
    shadow underneath.

Voila! Viscacha!

White-backed vulture

Gyps bengalensis
Africa. Size: 81 cm (32 inches);
wingspan 2.2 m (7 ft 3 in). Vultures are
scavengers. They clean up leftovers
from other animal's meals. With keen
eyesight, they soar high in the air
looking for their next meal. Vultures
poke their heads inside dead animals
to eat, and so have no feathers on their
head or neck—feathers there would
become a mess quickly!

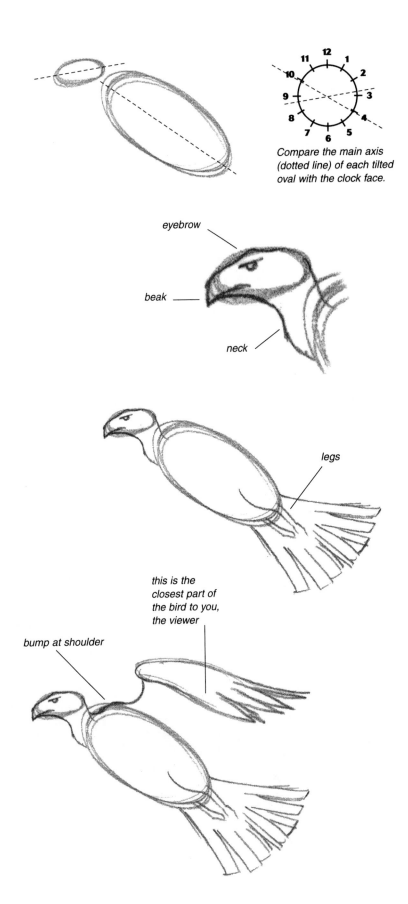

Compare the main axis
(dotted line) of each tilted
oval with the clock face.

eyebrow

beak

neck

legs

this is the
closest part of
the bird to you,
the viewer

bump at shoulder

1. Lightly draw two ovals, for
   the body and the head of
   the vulture.

   *Which is bigger? How much
   bigger? How is each oval
   tilted?*

2. With a sharp pencil, lightly
   outline the details of the
   head, and add the eye—a
   short straight line with a
   curved line underneath it.
   Add curved lines for the top
   and bottom of the neck.

3. At the other end of the large
   body oval, sketch the tail
   feathers fanning outward.
   Add the legs.

4. Above the body, lightly
   sketch the part of the wing
   that is coming toward you.
   This is a complicated shape,
   so draw very lightly at first,
   and do it again if you need
   to. Connect this shape to
   the body with a short curved
   line, running into a bump at
   the shoulder.

Always draw lightly at first!

5. Look at the dotted line. Compare it to the clock face on the opposite page. Now lightly draw the gently curving line of the top of the wing. Add the curving bottom part on both wings.

Sharpen your pencil. Carefully draw the feathers, radiating from the end of the wing, then closer together and parallel as they get closer to the body.

Clean up the outline of your vulture, erasing any smudges. Darken the wing and tail feathers, leaving the main part of each wing lighter. Add short pencil strokes to shade the wings, head, and body.

Clean up any smudges with your eraser.

Great venturous vulture!

Warthog

Phacochoerus aethiopicus
Africa. Size: 1.5–2 m (5–7.5 ft). The warthog gets its name from two wart-like bumps on each side of its face. Warthogs like to stay around water. They live in family groups and eat grass, fruit, and sometimes small mammals or dead animals. They can run up to 55 kph (35 mph), and raise their tails when alarmed. They burrow with their teeth, kneel on their calloused knees, and rest in crevices near trees and boulders where they're easy to (almost) step on.

Always draw lightly at first!

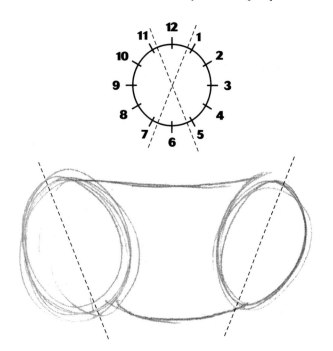

1) Draw two tilted ovals, connected with slightly curved lines.

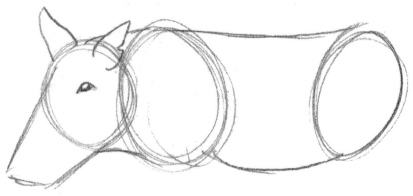

2) Add a light circle, slightly overlapping one of the ovals (not much of a neck on this pup). Extend the face downward, add eye and ears.

eyebrow

'warts'

3) At the end of the face, draw two sets of curving tusks. Add two 'warts' and the eyebrows. On the closer side of the face, draw the bump (wart) near the eye, and a crescent shadow for the bump closer to the nose. Add ears, and wrinkles under the chin.

Since this 'wart' is pointing at you, you see only its shadow

4) With small ovals at the joints, sketch the legs. Pay attention to the angles, and notice which parts of the legs are hidden by other parts of the body.

5) Go over the outline to clarify lines and add emphasis. With strong, quick strokes, add the wild bristly hair of the mane. Draw the tail.

6) Patiently shade the entire body *(notice the very few areas left white in this drawing)*. As you shade, turn your drawing so the pencil strokes help make the side of the warthog look cylindrical, or rounded. Add more wrinkles around the neck and eyes, and darker shading for the muscles of the rear leg. Draw a cast shadow on the ground.

Keep your hand off the drawing to avoid smudging. If you do make smudges, clean them with your eraser.

Give your warthog a name, preferably starting with a W.

Blue Wildebeest

Connochaetes taurinus
Africa. Size: 2.3–3.4 m (7.5–11 ft)
Wildebeests live in large herds, feeding on grass and often seen among zebras and ostriches. They are prey of lions, cheetahs, hunting dogs and hyenas. The Blue Wildebeest is also known as the Brindled Gnu. That was gnus to me, but I'll bet you gnu it already.

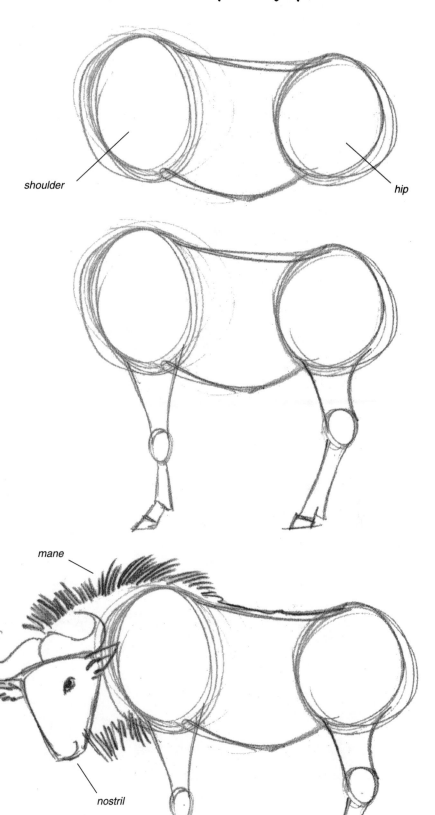

shoulder

hip

mane

nostril

1) Draw two light, almost-round ovals, one for the shoulder and the other for the hip. Connect the tops to make the back of the wildebeest, and the bottoms to make the stomach.

2) Add a front and rear leg, drawing lightly at first. Pay close attention to the angle of each segment of the legs. Add the hooves.

3) Lightly outline the head, roughly a triangle, with the top at the center of the shoulder. Add ears, sticking straight out to the side, the eye and the slit of the nostril. Carefully draw the curving horns on top of the head. Draw the mane, using short, repeated pencil strokes up from the neck. Do the same at the bottom of the neck, making strokes downward.

4) Lightly draw the other front and rear leg. Add the tail. Looking ahead to the finished drawing, notice which areas are darkest. Begin shading those areas first. Darken the bottom of the neck with more short, vertical pencil strokes.

5) Continue shading, using short pencil strokes. Add shading and grass underneath. Clean up any smudges with your eraser.

Cape Zebra

Equus zebra zebra (go ahead, memorize this one!)
Africa. Size: 1.3 m (4.2 ft) high at shoulder. These endangered zebras came close to extinction in the 1940s. The main threat was habitat loss, when water holes were cut off by fencing for livestock. About 450 now survive.

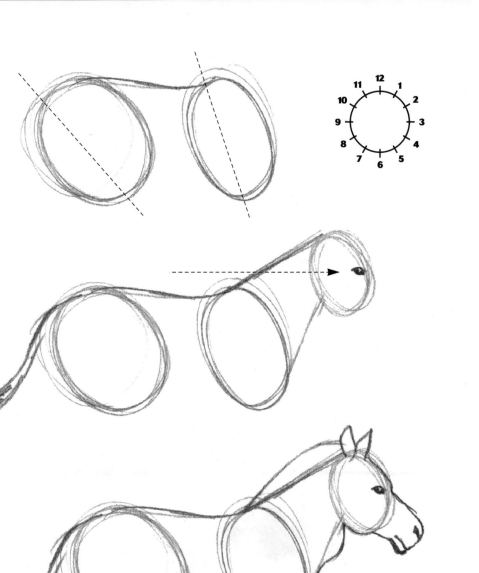

1) Lightly sketch two tilted ovals. Look at the clock face to make sure you have them tilting like the example. Connect them with a curvy line for the back.

2) Add the tail (easy!). At the opposite end, draw a light oval for the head (again, notice the tilt of the oval). At the very front of the oval, draw the eye. Notice where it lies in relation to the shoulder (above it). Draw the two lines of the neck.

3) Add ears, a light outline of the mane, a bulge at the throat, and a snout, complete with nostril and mouth. *Draw lightly until you're sure you have it right!*

4) Lightly sketch the legs, using light ovals at each joint to help you understand how the leg bends. The rear leg bends in three places. Look at the clock face and compare angles if you find part of it confusing.

Always draw lightly at first!

5) Ah, what a difference we see in this drawing! Add the two further legs, lightly at first, observing angles and joints carefully. Lightly erase the ovals—while helpful in getting the drawing started, we don't want them to show through the stripes!

(You did start out lightly, didn't you?)

6) Add stripes and shading, and curving pencil strokes for grass. Be sure to sharpen your pencil when you draw details. Also use a sharp pencil to lightly draw the pattern of the stripes before you darken them. Avoid smudging by keeping your hand off parts you've already drawn. Put a clean piece of paper under your hand to protect drawn areas, or turn the paper around so that your hand is on the white part while you draw.

Another thought: you might want to finish this drawings with a black colored pencil, which will smear less than a normal graphite pencil.

About those stripes: *the lone zebra above seems like a pretty obvious target for a hungry lion...but seen in a herd, it's not so easy to see where one zebra starts and another ends!*

Drawing tips

Lines make all the difference

Lines are not all created equal. Some lines can make your animal come to life. Try making your lines interesting. Learn to use lines to capture the feel of the animal you're drawing. Here are some suggestions:

The two baboons have the same shape. If both were on display, which would you want to be able to point to and say, "That's mine"?

✔ Make outlines interesting

Specifically, what parts of the outline make one drawing more interesting to look at than the other? Do you see a technique you can use in your drawing?

✔ Create texture with lines

Which drawing seems to have more texture–which drawing gives you an idea what the baboon might feel like if you touched it?

✔ Use lines to show form

In addition to showing texture, how do lines help show the form (form is three-dimensional shape)? Can you see areas on the baboon or hunting dog where lines make the drawing look more three-dimensional?

Drawing tips

Start out loose and light

You've seen it enough times throughout this book (I hope): *Always draw lightly at first.* Another way to say this would be *Always sketch at first.*

Sketching means trying out ideas, trying out variations, and basically not worrying too much whether the finished product is perfect.

This very light drawing, or sketching, makes it easier to learn to draw. Ideally, try to do a number of quick sketches to get a feel for the animal: from life, from pictures, or from videos or TV. Learn something from each sketch. Then carefully put together your final drawing, working more methodically and carefully.

You may find—as perhaps all illustrators and artists do—that your lightly drawn sketches have more energy, and capture more of the spirit of the animal, than your final drawing.

Welcome to the club!

Timed Drawings

When drawings are starting to get too tight, or too controlled, try this: pick a subject, and do timed drawings: first, **five seconds** (really, it's possible!). Next, do a 30-second drawing. One more: give yourself two minutes. Now take as long as you need—ten minutes, a half an hour, a day…feel the difference in each: which is the most fun?

One final thought...

Save your work!

Whenever you do a drawing–or even a sketch–put your initials (or autograph!) and date on it. And save it. You don't have to save it until it turns yellow and crumbles to dust, but do keep your drawings, at least for several months. Sometimes, hiding in your portfolio, they will mysteriously improve! I've seen it happen often with my own drawings, especially the ones I knew were no good at all, but kept anyway....

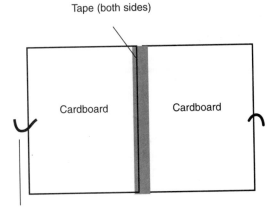

Tape (both sides)

Cardboard   Cardboard

String (to tie portfolio closed)

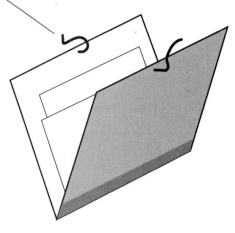

Do-it-yourself portfolio

Index

IF YOU'VE ENJOYED THIS BOOK, CHECK OUT SOME OF THE OTHERS!

Draw Rainforest Animals

Draw Desert Animals

Draw Ocean Animals

Draw Dinosaurs

Draw Cars

Draw Alien Fantasies

Draw Medieval Fantasies

Learn To Draw 3-D

...and more to come!

Check with better bookstores, or request a current catalog from:

Peel Productions
PO Box 546–R
Columbus, NC 28722-0546

Telephone (704) 894-8838
Fax (704) 894-8839

www.peelbooks.com

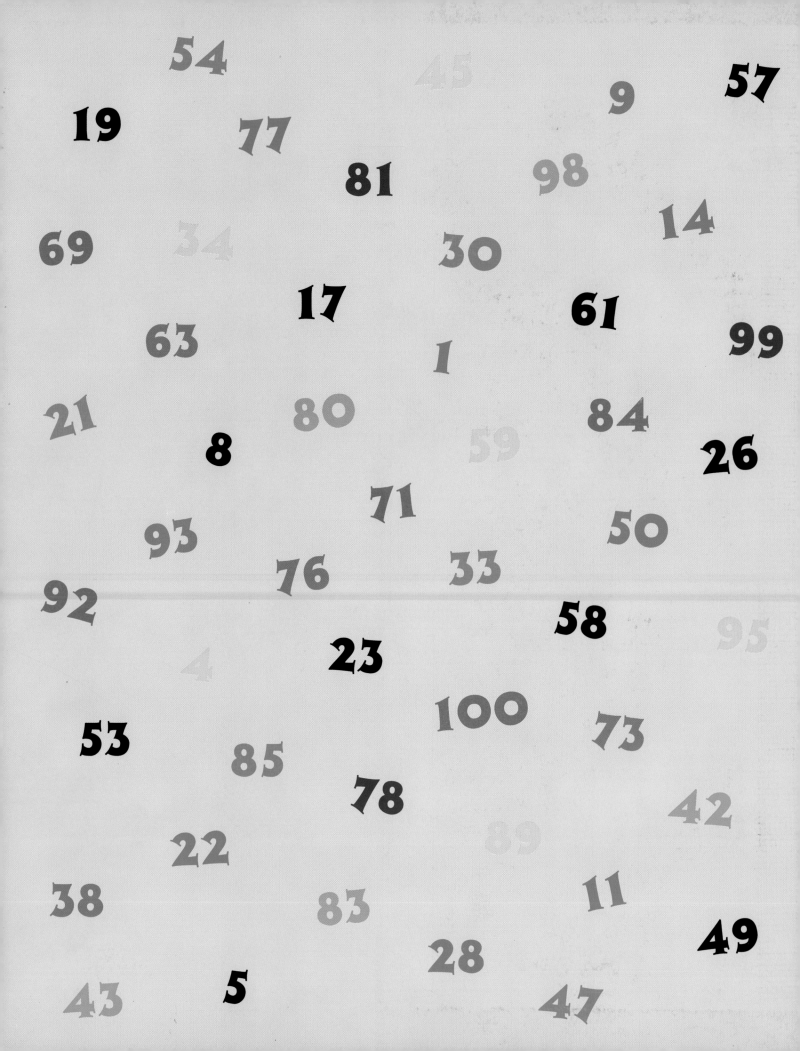

For Mickey, Mikey, Mark, Anna Maureen, and Annalea —J.S.

For Judy and Gerry, teachers and friends —A.W.

Our appreciation to Lynn Taylor, who introduced the celebration of 100 days in kindergarten in the 1981-82 Newsletter of the Center for Innovation in Education. Mrs. Taylor recently celebrated her 25th anniversary of teaching in primary grades in California and New Jersey. She was influenced by the late Mary Baratta-Lorton, whose theories on teaching children number concepts and math have been widely adopted. Mrs. Baratta-Lorton was director of early-childhood education at the California Center.—J.S. and A.W.

CIP Data is available.

Published in the United States 1998 by Dutton Children's Books, a member of Penguin Putnam Inc.
375 Hudson Street, New York, New York 10014
Designed by Amy Berniker · Printed in Hong Kong
First Edition   10 9 8 7 6 5 4 3 2 1
ISBN 0-525-46000-4

let's celebrate the 100th day!"

"Without more delay...

"Congratulations, kindergarten,"
says Miss Bindergarten.

Yolanda Pound and **Z**achary Blair boogie with their beads.

Wanda whoops and hollers.

Xavier shakes his seeds.

for the 100th day of kindergarten.

Now Miss Bindergarten is all ready

Ursula's bag is heavy, but **V**icki's bunch is light.

Sara checks her ant farm.

Tommy flies his kite.

Miss Bindergarten is *almost* ready for the 100th day of kindergarten.

Raffie lifts the lid up on one hundred dinosaurs.

Patricia sorts her crayons.

Quentin revs toy cars.

for the 100th day of kindergarten.

Miss Bindergarten gets ready

Ophelia's stuck with stickers from her hat down to her boots.

**Miss Bindergarten gets ready
for the 100th day of kindergarten.**

Lenny hugs a bagful of a hundred candy hearts.

Jessie pokes her polka dots.

Kiki carries tarts.

Miss Bindergarten gets ready for the 100th day of kindergarten.

Ian brings a relative
who's lived a hundred years.

Gwen creates a poster.

Henry claps and cheers.

for the 100th day of kindergarten.

Miss Bindergarten gets ready

Franny draws a picture of her hundred-year-old face.

The next morning—

Danny counts out cereal.

Emily fills a vase.

**Miss Bindergarten gets ready
for the 100th day of kindergarten.**

Brenda's
half asleep.

Christopher's
one hundred blocks
tumble in a heap.

That night—

Adam's fort is finished.

"100 days of friends, 100 days of fun,
100 days of darling, dazzling, winning work you've done.
So remember that tomorrow all of you must bring
100 of some wonderful, one-hundred-full thing!"

"**T**omorrow we celebrate," says Miss Bindergarten,
"the 100th day of kindergarten."

Miss Bindergarten Celebrates the 100th DAY

of Kindergarten

by **JOSEPH SLATE**

illustrated by **ASHLEY WOLFF**

Dutton Children's Books · New York

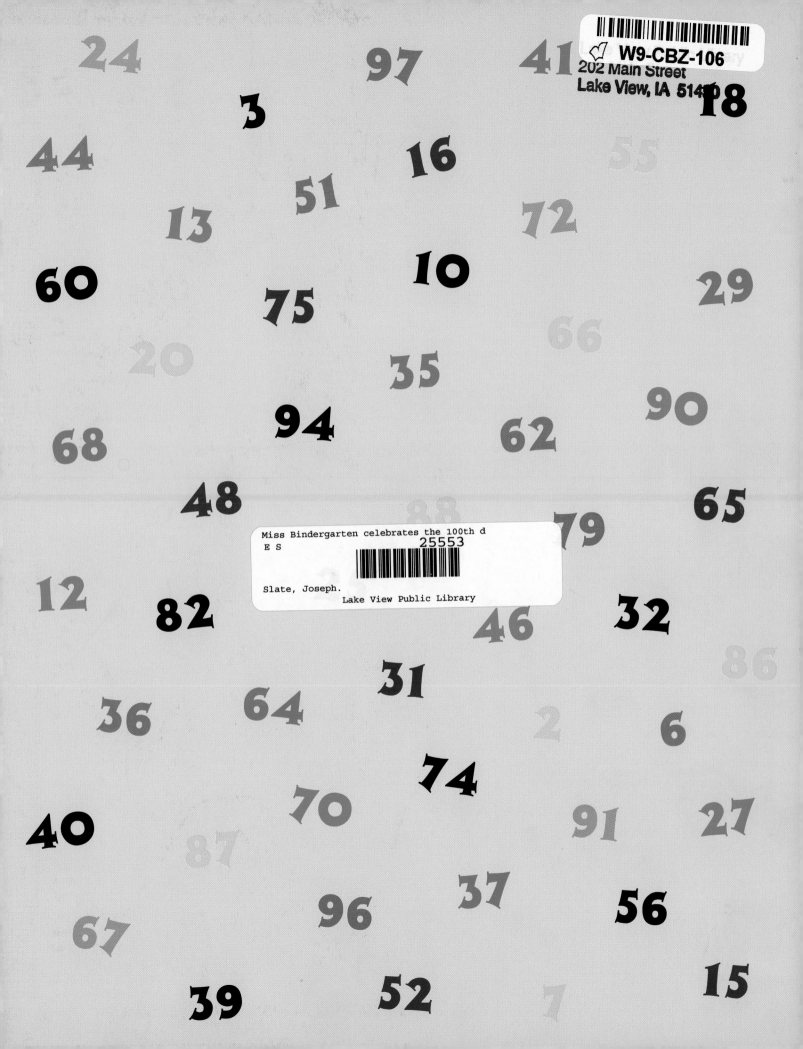